PATRICIA LEE GAUCH, EDITOR

PHILOMEL BOOKS
A division of Penguin Young Readers Group.
Published by The Penguin Group.
Penguin Group (USA) Inc., 375 Hudson Street, New York, NY 10014, U.S.A.
Penguin Group (Canada), 90 Eglinton Avenue East, Suite 700, Toronto,
       Ontario M4P 2Y3, Canada (a division of Pearson Penguin Canada Inc.).
Penguin Books Ltd, 80 Strand, London WC2R 0RL, England.
Penguin Ireland, 25 St. Stephen's Green, Dublin 2, Ireland (a division of Penguin Books
       Ltd).
Penguin Group (Australia), 250 Camberwell Road, Camberwell, Victoria 3124, Australia
       (a division of Pearson Australia Group Pty Ltd).
Penguin Books India Pvt Ltd, 11 Community Centre, Panchsheel Park, New Delhi - 110 017, India.
Penguin Group (NZ), 67 Apollo Drive, Rosedale, North Shore 0632, New Zealand
       (a division of Pearson New Zealand Ltd).
Penguin Books (South Africa) (Pty) Ltd, 24 Sturdee Avenue, Rosebank, Johannesburg 2196, South Africa.
Penguin Books Ltd, Registered Offices: 80 Strand, London WC2R 0RL, England.

Design by Semadar Megged.   The text is set in 15.5-point Galathea.
The illustrations are rendered in watercolors, gouache, and ink.
Library of Congress Cataloging-in-Publication Data
Gorbachev, Valeri.   Molly who flew away / Valeri Gorbachev.   p. cm.
Summary: Molly buys so many balloons for all her animal friends at
the fair, she gets carried away into the air.   [1. Fairs—Fiction.
2. Balloons—Fiction. 3. Animals—Fiction.] I. Title.
PZ7.G6475Mo 2009   [E]—dc22   2008032607

ISBN 978-0-399-25211-2
10 9 8 7 6 5 4 3 2 1

Molly
Who Flew Away

For my grandson, Avigdor.

Molly
Who Flew Away

Valeri Gorbachev

Philomel Books

Molly loved when the big fair came to town, because all of her friends went to the fair, too, and they could ride all the rides together.

Molly's friend Rabbit loved to laugh. Molly
loved to go into the fun house with him.

Molly's friend Goose was so adventurous.
Molly was adventurous, too! She loved to
ride the merry-go-round with Goose.

Molly's friend Frog was a real cowboy.
Molly hopped right up behind Frog. They rode
the ponies more than once.

Molly's friend Pig loved puppet shows. When
they discovered one at the fair, they sat through
two shows together.

Molly's friend Dog was so brave—he wasn't even afraid of riding the giant Ferris wheel! Molly felt so brave with Dog, they rode the wheel together, over and over.

Then, Molly remembered that her mother had given her some pocket change to buy herself some goodies. So, she ran off to look for goodies to buy.

"That's a nice jug," said Molly. "But I have one already."

"I could buy a doughnut," she said to herself, "but it's too big for me to eat alone."

"I could buy a game and play it with Rabbit and Goose!"

Suddenly, Molly saw some kids going by, holding wonderful, colorful balloons.

"I have a great idea," Molly said right out loud. "Colored balloons would make a great gift for my friends."

So Molly ran over to the balloon salesman with her pocket change in her hand.

"Please, Mr. Balloon Man," she said. "I would like
a pink balloon for my friend Pig,
a green balloon for my friend Frog,
a red polka dot balloon for my friend Rabbit
—I know he loves the color red!—
an orange balloon for my friend Goose,
a blue striped balloon for my friend Dog,
and . . ."

"a yellow balloon for me!" said Molly.

Suddenly, Molly's legs started to
lift right off the ground.
"Where are you going, little
one?" called the Balloon Man.

"The balloons are carrying me away!" cried Molly.

"Help me!"

"Somebody . . . catch me!"

"Save me!"

But no one could.

and over
the river.

Then she heard some voices
shouting, "We'll catch you, Molly!"
It was all of her friends—running
after her.

They ran through the meadow . . .

They ran up the hill.

And they caught her—just as she floated by.

"What an incredible flight!" they cried.
"Yes," said Molly. "But good thing I
have so many friends, or I'd still be flying!"

Then, she happily gave each of them a balloon of just the right color: a pink one for Pig, a green one for Frog, a red polka dot one for Rabbit, an orange one for Goose, a blue striped one for Dog . . .

and she saved the yellow one for herself.